Bumblegreen Books are committed to reducing climate change.

The not so Green Queen was printed using a 100% waterless process, in a factory powered by 100% renewable energies, that produces zero waste to landfill. This is important to us, and we believe, just as important to all of our readers.

Bumblegreen Books is committed to the environment.
This book is printed using processes that are:

100%	100%	100%	100%	100%	100%
waterless LED	alcohol and substitute free	carbon positive	renewable energy	recycled FSC® stock	VOC free inks

Zer 0 % waste to landfill

Printed by **seacourt** – proud to be counted amongst the top environmental printers in the world

Thank you to the wonderful Bumblegreen team, Mia and Georgia, and Bumblegreen friends, Branka and Smiljka.

To Rich

Published by Bumblegreen Books
First published 2020

This edition published 2020
Text and illustrations © Katherine Wheatley, 2020
Technical Designers Georgia Yates & Mia Buonaguro
Editor Jasmine Greaves
10 9 8 7 6 5 4 3 2 1

Printed in Great Britain by Seacourt
ISBN 978-0-9569693-1-6

In a very large castle, there lived a queen,

Who'd heard in the town that it was good to be green.

Green thought the Queen, how strange to be green!

I'll be the greenest queen this town has ever seen.

So she started work straight away,

And organised a *special* green day.

She sent invitations to all of the town,

And ordered a brand new,

emerald green crown.

Royal Invitation

To all the townsfolk you are hereby invited to a

GREEN BALL

When: Saturday
Time: 6 o'clock

Then...

She painted the castle, the walls and the floors.

She painted the chairs, the table and doors.

She even painted the toilet seat,

And covered the bed with a jazzy green sheet.

In the royal garden, she painted the flower tubs,
And filled the borders with evergreen shrubs.

She painted bright green swirls on the path,
And splattered the base of the old bird bath.

WET PAINT

And then she hung little, green lights,

In the beautiful trees to glow in the night.

The garden *twinkled* and *sparkled* brightly,

And at last the Queen sat down quietly.

She grinned with delight.
What a fabulous sight!

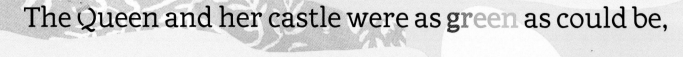

The Queen and her castle were as green as could be,

Ready for the people in the town to see.

The Queen was thrilled about being so green.

"I must be the greenest queen people have ever seen!"

On the day of the *ball*, when she awoke,

She started to get ready for all the townsfolk.

The Queen created a menu of dishes,

And the chef worked hard to meet her *wishes*.

All of this green is a bit extreme!

Royal mushy peas
mixed with minty leaves

Vegetable strips
delicious with dips

Lime green jellies
sprinkled with cherries

Cucumber spread
served on royal bread

A yummy, mouth-watering, green iced cake,

Which the chef was excited and proud to bake.

The menu's theme of course was...

not red, not yellow, not orange, not purple, not blue...

BUT...

Finally, the people gathered in the **huge**, green hall,
Ready for the Queen and her very green ball!

Welcome to my
special green day.
I have something very
important to say.

She announced to the town, "I'm the greenest queen around!"
And the people looked **amazed** and made a *giggling* sound.

The people stared and waited for a reply,

But the Queen just stood with her head held high.

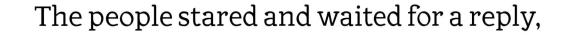

I AM VERY GREEN!
HOW DARE YOU DISAGREE!
Just look at the castle and look at me.

Being **green** is NOT just
a **colour** my dear.

It's all about the things we
do each day,
to make this **world** a better
place to stay.

Then one-by-one the people told the Queen,
About the things they did to try to be green.

When the people had finished, they said goodbye,

And the Queen 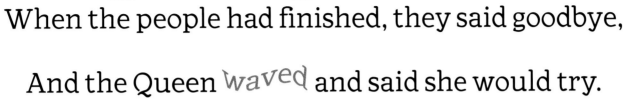 waved and said she would try.

How silly, how daft!
What was I thinking?
I really didn't have an inkling!

I'm going to have to make a PLAN!

Later that night,

when she lay in bed,

The things they said

went round in her head.

The very next day, she started to change her ways,

And the townsfolk didn't see her for days and days.

Monday 1

Thursday 18

Sunday 14

Friday 10

Tuesday

Sunday 27

Monday 29

August

M	T	W	T	F	S	S
Create a recycling Centre	Order new Trees	Remind all the Royal staff to switch off at the plug	Begin vegetable Patch	Order a Wind Turbine for the town		Collect bike and new helmet
Change to energy saving Light bulbs		Investigate how I can use less Plastic	Fit a new clothes line	Save Water	Create compost System	Investigate ECO friendly Palm Oil
	Plant new Trees	Create mini beast friendly zones		Investigate Bee-friendly Plants and add them to the Royal Garden		
Delivery and fixing of the new wind turbines	Send e-invites to townsfolk to re-visit the castle		Visit the Swap shop for new outfits for all the townsfolk		townsfolk to revisit the Castle!	

It was one month later, when finally they were invited,

To attend a special party - and they were very excited.

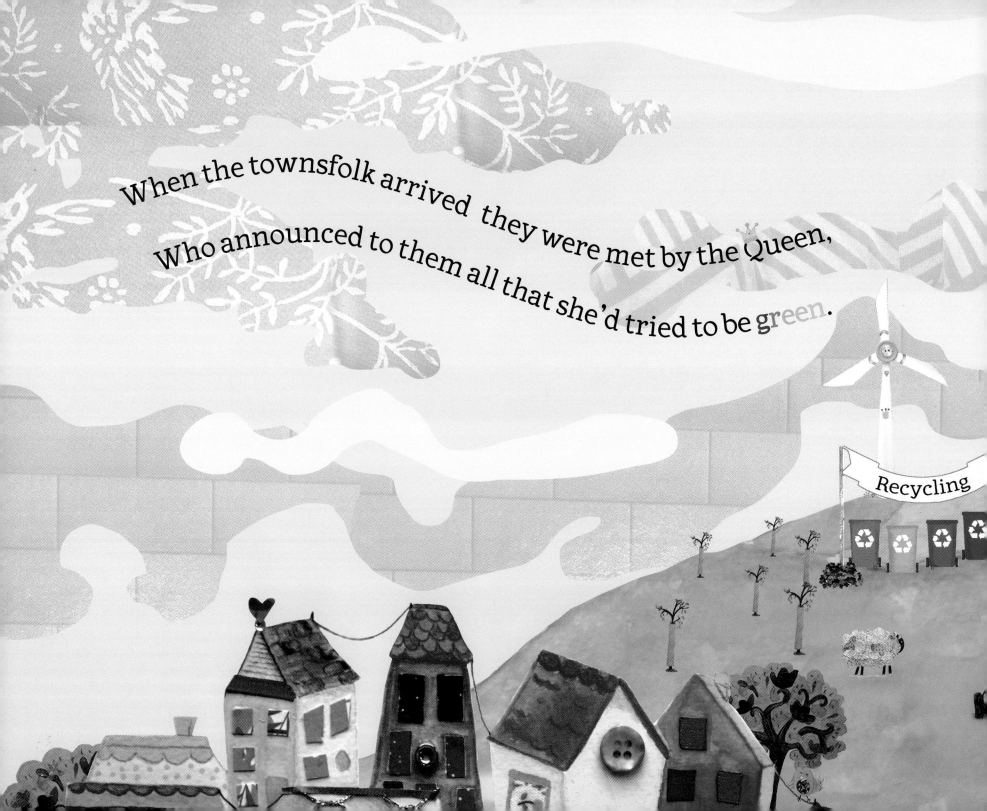

When the townsfolk arrived they were met by the Queen,

Who announced to them all that she'd tried to be green.

Recycling

Inside the castle...

Composting bins for royal teabags and peelings

Energy saving lightbulbs

Recycled toilet paper in the royal bathrooms

Reusable bags for the royal shopping

Bamboo toothbrushes
No more plastic

Reusable bottle for royal drinks

composting

Reusable water bottle

Royal Green Pledges...

Although the Queen

had only just begun,

She declared to them all,

that being green was...

FUN!

Pledge 1
Save water
Take shorter
showers

Pledge 2
Save energy
Switch OFF
at the plug

Pledge 3
Recycle and
Recreate
30-Wear
Pledge

Pledge 4
Shop Locally

Pledge 5
Cycle or Walk
for short
journeys

Pledge 6
Create more
Wildlife zones

The Mayor was **amazed** as the difference was clear,

And the townsfolk jumped and began to cheer.

There stood the Queen - she wasn't dressed in green,

But she certainly was the greenest queen

the town had **ever** seen.

Yes!

I like
her new
bike!

Hooray!

minibeast
hotel

Wow!
Such a BIG
difference.

As a *special* celebration for the Queen,

The townsfolk agreed that they'd all wear green.

So now once a year there's an ECO *ball*,

To celebrate planet Earth that belongs to us all.

Not red, not yellow, not blue, not pink

GREEN

...is the colour that makes you think!

Recycle, Reuse and Reduce your waste,
to make this world a much better place.

ECOLOGY is all about
the environment,
nature and habitats,
and how these are
linked
together.

ECO relates
to the word
ECOLOGY.

Choose to do things
that will help
protect and
look after our
wonderful
planet.

Being Eco-Friendly
means that we do not
harm the
environment.

One day the Queen hears in the town that it is good to be green and decides that she is going to be the greenest queen the town has ever seen.

How does she get this so wrong?

Find out how the townsfolk help the Queen understand what it really means to be green.

Bumblegreen

www.bumblegreenbooks.co.uk

UK £7.99

ISBN 978-0-9569693-1-6

9 780956 969316 >